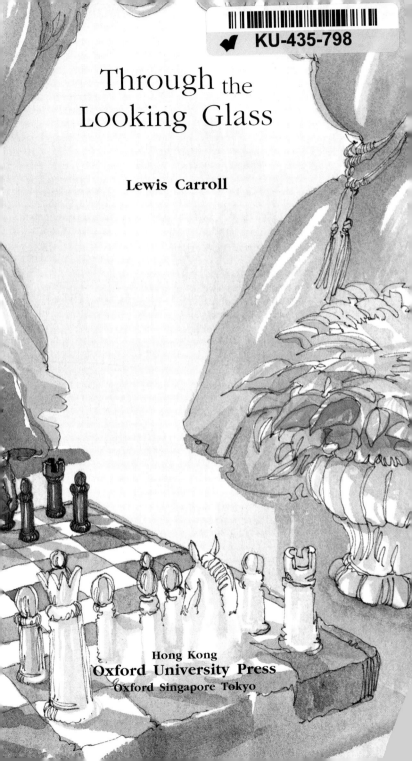

KU-435-798

Through the Looking Glass

Lewis Carroll

Hong Kong
Oxford University Press
Oxford Singapore Tokyo

Oxford University Press

Oxford　New York　Toronto
Kuala Lumpur　Singapore　Hong Kong　Tokyo
Delhi　Bombay　Calcutta　Madras　Karachi
Nairobi　Dar es Salaam　Cape Town
Melbourne　Auckland　Madrid

and associated companies in
Berlin　Ibadan

Oxford is a trade mark of Oxford University Press

First published 1992
Second impression 1994

© Oxford University Press 1992

Illustrated by K.Y.Chan

Syllabus designer: David Foulds

Text processing and analysis by Luxfield Consultants Ltd.

ISBN 0 19 585268 0

Printed in Hong Kong
Published by Oxford University Press (Hong Kong) Ltd
18/F Warwick House, Taikoo Place,
979 King's Road, Quarry Bay, Hong Kong

CONTENTS

1

THE LOOKING-GLASS HOUSE

Alice talks to the black kitten

Alice was sitting on a chair by the fire. She was watching the two little kittens playing with their mother.

Dinah (that was the mother cat) was washing the white kitten's face. First she held the little kitten down by its ear. Then she cleaned its face, beginning at the nose.

The black kitten had finished its wash. It was playing with a ball of wool.

'Oh, don't take my wool again,' said Alice. The kitten took one end of the ball of wool. It ran across the room until there was wool all over the floor. Then the kitten came back and sat down in front of the fire. It had wool all round its neck and all round its tail.

Alice jumped out of her chair. She picked up the little kitten and the wool, and then sat down in her chair again.

'What a naughty little kitten you are! Didn't Dinah teach you to be good?' said Alice. 'You have been a very naughty kitten today, haven't you! You made a noise when your mother washed your face. You pulled your little sister's tail twice. Now you have undone my ball of wool. So, what do you say about that, kitten?

'What was that?' Alice pretended that the kitten could talk to her. 'Your mother's paw went in your eye, did it? Well, when your mother washes your face, you should shut your eyes.

'Oh, I don't know how I am going to punish you,' she continued. 'Let me see. I won't do anything today.

No, I'll wait until next week. Then I must punish you one, two, three times.'

The chess-board

'Can you play chess, Kitty?' said Alice, still talking to the black kitten. 'I think you can. You were watching very carefully when we played just now.

'It's such a nice game, isn't it? Look. Here is the chess-board we play on, with its black and white squares. And here are the little pieces we play with. The pieces at this end are red. This is the King, this is the Queen, these little ones are the Pawns and these are the Castles. These pieces that look like horses are the Knights. All the pieces at the other end are the same, but they are white, remember.

'I'm sure you understand, don't you? When you watched us playing I thought you understood everything.

'You can be the Red Queen, Kitty. Sit up there.' Alice tried to make the little black kitten sit on the table. 'Now put your arms in front of you, just like the queen.'

Alice took the Red Queen off the chess-board and put it by the kitten. But the kitten couldn't hold its paws together like the Red Queen.

'No,' said Alice. 'That's not right. Look. I'm going to hold you up in front of the looking-glass so that you can see yourself. Now try. If you are not good, I'll put you *through* the looking-glass into the Looking-Glass House!'

The Looking-Glass House

That was the first time Alice had said anything about the Looking-Glass House. She decided to tell the kitten all about it.

'Now, just listen to me, Kitty, and don't talk so much,' she said. 'Look in the mirror. First, you can see a room. That's just the same as our room here, only the things go the other way.

'I can see most of it when I climb up on a chair. I can't see the bit just below the looking-glass. I *wish* I could. I want to know if they have a fire, like ours, in the winter. I know they have books like ours, but the words go the wrong way. I can't read their books.

'Wouldn't you like to live in the Looking-Glass House, Kitty? I'm sure they have very nice milk in there for you to drink. And look! You can just see their door. If we open our door a little, we can see out of their door a little.

'Oh, I wish we could go into the Looking-Glass House. I'm sure it has lots of beautiful things in it.

'I know, Kitty. Let's pretend we can go through the glass. Let's pretend we can climb into the Looking-Glass House.'

Alice put her hand on the mirror. The glass felt soft! Her hand moved through it!

Through the Looking-Glass

Alice put the little black kitten down and climbed up in front of the mirror. The glass *was* beginning to change. It was like a cloud. Then Alice walked through the glass. She jumped down into the Looking-Glass room on the other side.

The first thing she did was to look and see if there was a fire. Yes, there *was* one. It was burning just as brightly as the one she had left behind.

'Oh, I shall be nice and warm here,' Alice thought. 'And it will be such fun. When they see me through the glass in here, they won't be able to touch me.'

Then Alice began to look about. Things looked the same as they did on the other side of the mirror. But no. Not quite the same. The pictures on the wall next to the fire seemed to be alive. And the clock had the face of a little old man who was smiling at her.

Suddenly, Alice noticed some chess pieces on the floor. She looked more closely at them. They were moving about. They were alive!

'Here are the Red King and the Red Queen,' Alice said very quietly, because she didn't want to frighten them. 'And there are the White King and the White Queen. Over there are two Castles. I don't think they can hear me. And I don't think they can see me either.'

Alice helps the Queen

Just then Alice heard a noise. It came from the table. It sounded like a little baby crying. She saw a white Pawn lying on the table, kicking and making a funny noise.

'It is my child,' said the White Queen, who was down on the floor. She hurried over to the table and began to climb up one of the table-legs.

Alice wanted to do something to help. She took the Queen in her fingers. She picked her up, and put her down again on the table by her little daughter.

The Queen got such a fright! She couldn't see Alice. She did not know that Alice had lifted her up. She thought perhaps it was the wind. She called out to the King, 'Be careful! There is a very strong wind today. It blew me right up here.'

'Strong wind? Fiddlesticks!' said the King, who never believed anything the Queen said. He started climbing up the table-leg.

'It will take you hours and hours to get up to the top, won't it?' said Alice. 'Let me help you.'

The King didn't say anything. He couldn't see or hear Alice. So Alice lifted him up carefully. The King found himself being carried slowly through the air. He did not know what was happening. His eyes got larger and larger. His mouth got rounder and rounder. It made Alice laugh to see him. She put him on the table near the Queen.

'Oh, please don't make a face like that!' Alice laughed.

'You will not believe what just happened to me,' said the King to the Queen. 'That is something I will never, never forget.'

'You *will* forget it,' said the Queen, 'if you don't write it down somewhere.'

The King took a large notebook from his pocket, and began to write in it.

Alice goes out

'Oh!' thought Alice, jumping up. 'If I don't hurry, I will have to go back through the Looking-Glass. I want to see the rest of the house, and I do want to have a look at the garden!'

So Alice ran out of the room. She started to run down the stairs. But she soon found she wasn't *running* down the stairs at all. Her feet didn't even touch the stairs. She was floating; floating through the air. It felt *very* strange. She floated right down to the front door.

She was feeling quite ill with so much floating through the air. So she held on to the door, and pulled herself to the ground. She was glad to find that she could walk again.

THE GARDEN OF TALKING FLOWERS

In the garden

Alice stepped out into the garden. She could not see very much. 'I will be able to see better,' said Alice to herself, 'if I go to the top of that hill. Here's a path that goes straight towards it.' ₅

Alice walked along the path. But it did not go straight to the hill. First it turned left. Then it turned right. Then it came *back* to the house. 'Well, I'll try to get to the hill another way,' said Alice.

And so she tried a different way. She walked up and down. She turned left and right. She tried this way and that way. But each time she came back to the house. ₁₀

'I'm not going inside yet,' said Alice. If I do, I will have to go through the Looking-Glass again — back into the old room. Then I will have no more fun.' ₁₅

So she turned around again and started walking along the path. 'I won't stop trying until I come to the hill,' she said.

Talking flowers

For a few minutes everything seemed well. But just when she thought she was at the hill, the path turned around again and she found herself walking in at the front door. 'Why does this house always get in my way!' said Alice. ₂₀

She started off again. This time she came to a large flower garden. There was a big flower at the ₂₅

edge of the garden. Alice had seen flowers like that before. It was a Tiger-Lily. Alice turned to the flower and said, 'Oh Tiger-Lily, I *wish* you could talk.'

'We can talk,' said the Tiger-Lily, 'when there is
5 somebody to talk to.'

Alice was so surprised, she couldn't speak. But then after a minute she asked, 'Can *all* the flowers here talk?'

'We can talk as well as you can,' said the Tiger-Lily.

'But we don't like to be the first to speak,' said the
10 Rose. 'It isn't polite. I was waiting for you to speak. I said to myself, "*Her* face doesn't look *too* stupid. Though I wouldn't say she was clever. But she *is* the right colour."'

'Her colour is not important,' said the Tiger-Lily. 'But
15 I don't like her leaves.'

'I have never seen anyone look so silly,' said a little blue flower. 'She's not like a real flower at all!'

'Be quiet!' said the Tiger-Lily.
'How would you know what a
20 real flower looks like? Go
back to sleep!'

Then all the
flowers began
talking together.
25 They were all
talking about
Alice, and
she didn't
like it.

'Be quiet everyone!' said the Tiger-Lily, moving angrily from side to side.

'Yes, be quiet,' said Alice, 'or I will pick you all!'

At once there was silence. Some of the pink flowers turned white.

'I've been in many gardens before, but none of the flowers could talk,' said Alice

'Put your hand down, and feel the ground,' said the Tiger-Lily. 'Then you'll know why.'

Alice touched the ground. It was very hard.

'You see,' said the Tiger-Lily, 'in most gardens, the flower beds are too soft, so the flowers are always asleep.'

'Oh, I didn't think of that!' said Alice. 'Are there any more people in the garden?' she asked.

'There is *one* other flower in the garden that can move about like you,' said the Rose. 'And I cannot *think* how you *do* that,' she whispered to herself.

'You can never think of anything!' said the Tiger-Lily.

'Is the other flower like me?' asked Alice. Perhaps there was another little girl in the garden somewhere.

'Well, she has the same funny *shape* as you,' said the Rose, 'but she is *redder* , and her leaves are longer. You might see her soon. Yes, look. *There* she is now.'

Alice looked round. It was the Red Queen. But she was much bigger. When Alice first saw her inside the house, she was only a few centimetres high. Now she was taller than Alice.

Alice meets the Red Queen

Alice wanted to talk to the Queen, so she walked towards her. To her surprise the Queen disappeared. In a few minutes Alice was walking in at the front door of the Looking-Glass House again. She turned around, and saw the Queen a long way away.

Then Alice remembered she was in the Looking-Glass world. Everything was the wrong way round. She thought she would try walking in the opposite direction.

She did not have to walk far before she found the Red Queen. She was also close to the hill she had seen.

'Where do you come from?' said the Red Queen. 'Where are you going? Look up, girl. Stand up straight. Speak nicely.'

Alice started to tell the Queen that she was trying to get to the hill. She said she had lost her way. The Queen said, 'Lost your way? What do you mean? All the ways here belong to me. You do not have any ways so you cannot lose one! But why are you here?'

'I wanted to see the garden,' said Alice.

'Garden, you say!' said the Queen, 'This is not a garden. *I* can show you gardens which make *this* place look like a desert.'

'And I wanted to get to the top of that hill,' said Alice.

'Hill, you say!' said the Queen, 'That's not a hill. *I* can show you hills which make *that* place look like a valley.'

'But a hill can't be a valley,' said Alice. 'That is nonsense.'

The Red Queen looked at her. 'Nonsense, you say,' she said, 'That's not nonsense. *I've* heard nonsense which makes *my* words seem as clever as a dictionary.'

Alice didn't want to make the Queen angry, so she didn't say anything more. She and the Queen walked together to the top of the hill.

For some minutes she stood without speaking. She looked in all directions over the country. It was a strange place, she thought. There were little streams crossing it everywhere, dividing the ground into squares. It was just like a big chess-board.

'There must be some chess-men moving out there,' she said to herself. 'Yes, I think I can see them. It's a big game of chess that is being played all over the world, if this is the world. What fun it is! I would like to join in the game. It would be nice to be a Pawn, but I would like best to be a Queen!'

Alice runs with the Queen

Just then, Alice and the Queen started to run. Alice didn't remember how it started. Suddenly she found she was holding the Queen's hand. The Queen went so fast that it was difficult for Alice to run with her. 'Faster! Faster!' the Queen shouted.

The strange thing was that nothing round them changed as they ran. They never seemed to pass anything.

'Is everything moving along with us as we run?' Alice asked herself.

'Faster! Don't try to talk!' said the Queen.

'Are we nearly there?' Alice asked the Queen.

'Are we nearly there!' the Queen repeated. 'We passed it ten minutes ago. Faster!' They ran on, with the wind blowing past Alice's ears and almost pulling her hair off.

'Now, Now!' shouted the Queen. 'Faster! Faster!' They went so fast they seemed to fly through the air, not touching the ground with their feet. Then they stopped, and Alice sat down on the ground with her head in her hands. The Queen sat against a tree and said, 'You may rest a little now.'

Alice looked around her. She was surprised to see they were still in the place where they had started running!

'But have we been under this same tree all the time? Everything is just the same as it was before.'

'Of course,' said the Queen.

'But in my country,' said Alice, 'if you run very fast for a very long time, like we did, then you arrive somewhere else!'

'That must be a very slow country,' said the Queen. 'Now here, you see, you must run as fast as you can, just to stay in the same place. If you want to get somewhere else, you must run twice as fast as that.'

The Queen gives Alice her directions

The Queen turned to Alice and said, 'Now I shall give you your directions. A Pawn begins on the second square, you know. And it moves two squares in its first move. You will go very quickly through the third square, by train I think. You will soon be in the fourth square. That square belongs to Tweedledum and Tweedledee. The Fifth square is quite wet. The sixth square belongs to Humpty Dumpty. Have you got anything to say?'

'No,' said Alice. Alice wasn't sure what was happening, but she guessed she was going to play a game of chess.

'The seventh square,' the Queen went on, 'is full of trees. It is all forest. Someone will show you the way through. In the eighth square, we shall all be Queens together.'

'Speak in French when you don't know what to say in English,' the Queen continued. 'Walk with your toes pointing out. Remember who you are. Goodbye.' The Queen did not wait for Alice to reply. One minute she was there, talking to Alice, and the next, she was gone.

Alice was now a Pawn. It was time for her to begin the game.

THE THIRD SQUARE

Alice begins her travels

Alice ran down the hill and jumped over the first of
six little streams.

She was in a train!

'Tickets, please,' said a man standing by the train.   5
'I'm the Guard. Show me your tickets.' He put his head
inside the window. 'Tickets! Tickets!' Everyone held
out a ticket. The tickets were about the same size as
the people, and almost filled the train.

'Where is your ticket, child?' said the Guard,   10
looking at Alice. All the people said together, 'Yes,
where is your ticket, child?'

'I'm sorry, I haven't got one,' replied Alice. She was
beginning to feel frightened. 'There wasn't a ticket office
where I came from.'   15

'There wasn't a ticket office where she came from!'
the voices repeated.

'Why didn't you buy one from the driver?' said
the Guard. The Guard looked at her very carefully.
'You are going the wrong way,' he said. He shut the   20
window and walked away.

'You should know where you are going, even if you
don't know your name,' said an old man. He was sitting
opposite Alice. His clothes were made of white paper.

A goat was sitting next to the old man. The goat   25
said in a loud voice, 'You should know how to get a
ticket, even if you can't read!'

It was a very strange train. Everyone in it wanted
to talk at the same time.

'She'll have to go back inside a bag!'   30

'That sounds like a horse talking,' Alice thought.

'She'll have to go by post,' said another. And someone else said, 'She'll have to pull the train all by herself!'

5 But the man wearing white said, 'Don't listen to them. Buy a return ticket every time the train stops.'

'No, I won't!' said Alice. 'I don't know how I got on to this train. I was standing on a hill just now. I wish 10 I could get back there!'

Alice finds a friend

Then she heard a very small voice close to her ear. Was it the voice of an insect?

15 'I know you are a friend,' said the little voice. 'You are a good friend. You won't hurt me just because I am a little insect.'

'What kind of insect are you?' Alice asked. She looked around to see who was talking to her. But 20 then the train made a very loud noise and everyone jumped up in fright.

The horse looked out of the window. He said, 'It's only a stream. We must jump over.' Everyone sat down again.

Alice wasn't sure if she wanted to stay in the train. Then she thought, 'Well, it will take us into the fourth square.' 5

She was thinking, 'How does a train jump over a stream?' when she felt the train go up into the air. She got such a fright. She put out her hand to hold on to something, and took hold of the goat. 10

But when they passed over the stream, the goat and the train and everyone else was gone.

A bad joke

Alice found herself sitting under a tree. The fly (the insect she had been 15 talking to) was sitting on a branch above her head.

It had become a very large fly. It was almost as big as a chicken, 20 Alice thought. But since it was a friendly insect, she felt quite happy.

'Do you like all insects?' the fly asked.

'I like them when they can talk,' Alice said. 'None of them ever talk where I come from.'

'Well, they cannot be real insects if they can't talk, can they?' said the fly.

'I don't know,' said Alice. 'But I know their names.'

'Do they come when you call their names?' asked the fly.

'I don't think so,' said Alice.

'So, why do they have names, then?' asked the fly.

'It's not useful to them,' said Alice, 'but it's useful to us.'

'They don't have names in the wood down there,' said the fly. It was looking across the field in front of them. On the far side there was a large, dark group of trees. 'Nothing in that wood has a name. Would you like to lose your name?'

'No, I wouldn't,' said Alice.

'But think,' replied the fly, 'it would be very useful. If the teacher wanted to call you to the front of your class, she would say "Come here …" Then she would have to stop because there wouldn't be any name. And so you wouldn't have to go.'

'But if she couldn't remember my name,' said Alice, 'she would say "Miss".'

'Well, if she said "Miss", you could *miss* your lesson!' said the fly.

'Oh, that's a very bad joke!' said Alice.

The fly made a sad little noise. Then when Alice looked up at the branch there was nothing on it. The fly had gone.

Alice goes into the wood

Alice walked on. Soon she came to the field with the wood on the other side of it. The wood looked dark, and Alice was quite frightened to go through it. But then she said, 'No, I must go on. This is the only way to the eighth square, and I don't want to go back.'

As she walked across the field towards the wood she thought, 'This must be the place where things have no names. What will happen to my name when I go in? I *don't* want to lose it. If I do, they will give me another name, and I don't want an ugly name. But then it would be fun to look for the person who has my old name.'

When Alice reached the wood it did not seem to be so dark. It looked nice and cool. 'Oh, this is nice,' said Alice, 'To be able to stand in the — in the what?' But she couldn't find the word she wanted. 'I mean, to walk in this — this. I mean, to sit under this — this, you know.' She put out her hand and touched a tree. What does it call itself? Perhaps it doesn't have a–a–a. Oh!'

Alice forgets her name

Alice stood quietly for a minute thinking. Then she suddenly began again. 'Then it really has happened. And now, who am I? I will remember, if I can. Yes, I will remember.'

But this didn't help. She couldn't remember anything at all.

Just then a deer came walking out of the forest. It looked at Alice with its big friendly eyes. It wasn't frightened at all to see her. 'Come here. Come here,' said Alice, as she held out her hand and tried to touch it. It only stepped back a little and stood looking at her again.

'What do you call yourself?' the deer asked Alice, with a very soft and sweet voice.

'I wish I knew,' thought poor Alice. She answered, quite sadly, 'Nothing, just now.'

'Think again,' it said.

Alice thought, but nothing came to her. 'Please tell me what *you* call yourself,' she said to the deer.

'I'll tell you, if we walk some more,' said the deer. 'I can't remember here.'

So they walked on together through the forest. Alice put her arms round the deer's neck until they came out into another field. Here the deer jumped suddenly into the air and said, 'Oh, I'm a deer. And *you* are a child.' It ran away quickly, back into the wood.

The path with two signs

Alice stood watching it. She was sad to lose her new friend so quickly. Then she thought, 'Well, now I know my name. *Alice. Alice.* I won't ever forget it again. Where shall I go now?'

That was not a very difficult question to answer. In front of her there was a forest, and there was only one path through it.

On the side of the path there were two signs. They both pointed in the same direction. One had TO TWEEDLEDUM'S HOUSE written on it. The other sign said TO TWEEDLEDEE'S HOUSE. Alice walked on along the path.

'They must both live in the same house,' said Alice, 'because both the signs point in the same direction. I won't stay there long. I'll just say "How do you do?" and ask them the way out of the forest. I must get to the eighth square before it gets dark.'

She walked on and on down the path, talking to herself as she went. Then she turned a corner and suddenly saw two fat little men. Alice was surprised. She stepped back, but when she looked at them again she knew who they must be.

TWEEDLEDUM AND TWEEDLEDEE

Alice asks the way

They were standing under a tree, each with an arm round the other's neck. Alice knew which was Tweedledum and which was Tweedledee. One of them had DUM on the front of his shirt, ₅ and the other had DEE. 'They must have TWEEDLE written at the back,' thought Alice.

They stood so still that ₁₀ Alice almost forgot they were alive. She looked round to see if the word TWEEDLE was written at the back of each shirt. Then she heard a voice coming from DUM. 'We weren't made just to be looked at, you know!'

And then the other one said, 'If you want to see if we are alive, then you should say something to us.'

'Oh, I'm sorry!' said Alice politely. 'I was thinking about how to get out of this forest. It's getting very dark. Can you tell me, please?'

But the fat little men just looked at each other and smiled. Then they held out their hands and said, 'How do you do?'

Alice did not want to make either of them angry, so she took both of their hands at the same time. Suddenly they were all dancing around in a circle.

The other two soon became tired, because they were so fat. 'Four times round is enough for one dance,' said Tweedledum. They both stopped dancing just as quickly as they had started.

The poem

They let go of Alice's hands and stood looking at her. There was a short silence. Alice wasn't sure how to begin a conversation with people she had just been dancing with. She couldn't say, 'How do you do?' now, she thought to herself. Then after a few minutes she said, 'I hope you are not too tired.'

'No, we are not. And thank you very much for asking,' said Tweedledee.

'You are *very* kind,' said Tweedledum. 'Do you like poetry?'

'I like *some* poetry,' said Alice. 'But could you tell me how to get out of this forest, please?'

'Which poem shall we do?' Tweedledee asked Tweedledum.

'"*The Walrus and The Carpenter*" is the longest poem we know,' Tweedledum replied.

Then Tweedledee began:

'The sun was shining on the sea,
Shining with all his might,
He did his best to make the waves
Look smooth and flat and bright,
And this was strange, because it was   5
The middle of the night.

The moon was watching angrily,
Because she thought the sun
Should not be in the sky at all
After the day was done,   10
"It's very rude of him," she said,
"To come and spoil the fun."

The sea was wet as wet can be,
The sand was dry as dry,
You could not see a cloud because   15
No cloud was in the sky.
No birds were flying through the air,
There were no birds to fly.

The Walrus and the Carpenter,
Were walking hand in hand,   20
They cried because it hurt to see
Such large amounts of sand.
"If this could just be swept away,"
They said, "we'd see the land."

"If seven girls with seven brooms,   25
Swept it for half a year,
Do you believe," the Walrus said,
"That they would get it clear?"
"I think so," said the Carpenter,
And cried another tear.   30

"Oh Oysters, come," the Walrus said,
"Along the sandy shore:
A little walk, a little talk,
We'd love to know you more:
We'll hold your hands and help you go,
We can't take more than four."

The oldest Oyster looked at him,
But not a word he said:
The oldest Oyster closed one eye,
And shook his heavy head,
Meaning to say he did not choose
To leave the Oyster-bed.

But four young Oysters hurried up,
They looked so nice to meet,
Their coats were brushed, their faces washed,
Their shoes were clean and neat,
And this was strange because, you know,
They hadn't any feet!

Four other Oysters followed them,
And soon another four,
Little ones and bigger ones,
And more and more and more,
They left the sea, they left the rocks,
And hurried to the shore.

The Walrus and the Carpenter,
Walked for an hour or so,
And then they saw some big flat rocks,
And sat down nice and low,
Then all the little Oysters stood,
And waited in a row.

"The time has come," the Walrus said,
"To talk of many things,
Of shoes and ships and shopkeepers,
Of cabbages and Kings,
And why the sea is much too hot,   5
And whether pigs have wings."

"A loaf of bread," the Walrus said,
"Yes, that is what we need,
And let's have pepper and some salt:
They're very good indeed,   10
Now if you're ready, Oysters, dear,
We can begin to feed."

"But don't eat us!" the Oysters said,
Turning a little blue,
"To eat us isn't very nice,   15
 It's not the thing to do."
"The night is fine," the Walrus said,
"And do you like the view?"

"It was so kind of you to come!"
The friendly Walrus said,
The Carpenter just sighed and cut
Another piece of bread.
5   *"I wish you wouldn't talk so much.*
Sit down and eat, instead!"

"It's really sad," the Walrus said,
"To play them such a trick.
We made them walk so very far,
10   *And run so very quick."*
The Carpenter could only say,
"This bread is nice and thick!"

"I cry for you," the Walrus said,
"You should have been more wise,"
15   *But as he cried he lifted up*
Those of the largest size,
And held a large white handkerchief
Before his sad blue eyes.

"O, Oysters," said the Carpenter,
20   *"You've had a lovely run,*
Shall we get ready to go home?"
But answer – there was none,
And this was not surprising, for
They'd eaten every one!'

THE RED KING

The King is sleeping

'I liked the Walrus best,' said Alice, 'because he said he was sorry for the oysters.'

'He ate more than the Carpenter,' said Tweedledee. 'Do you remember how he held up his handkerchief? That was so the Carpenter couldn't see how many he ate.'

'Oh, yes, that's right,' said Alice. 'Then I like the Carpenter best — if he didn't eat so many as the Walrus.'

'But he ate as many as he could get,' said Tweedledum.

Alice thought for a few minutes, then she said, 'Well I don't really like *either* of them!'

Just as she spoke, she heard something that sounded like a train. It was in the forest near where they were standing. She was afraid it might be a dangerous animal.

'Are there any lions in this forest?' she asked.

'It's only the Red King. He makes that noise when he sleeps,' said Tweedledee.

'Come and look at him,' the brothers said. They each took one of Alice's hands and led her to the place where the King was sleeping.

'Look at him!' they said.

He looked very funny to Alice. He had a tall, red hat on his head, and he was lying with his knees up in front of him.

'It isn't good for him to sleep on the grass like this,' said Alice.

'He's dreaming now,' said Tweedledee. 'And what do you think he is dreaming about?'

'I don't know,' said Alice.

Dream people

'He is dreaming about *you*,' said Tweedledee. 'And if
he suddenly stopped dreaming about you, where do
you think you would be?'

'Where I am now, of course,' said Alice.

'No, you wouldn't,' replied Tweedledee angrily.
'You would be nowhere. You are only a thing in his
dream.'

'Yes,' said Tweedledum. 'If the King wakes up —
you'll go away.'

'I *won't*,' said Alice loudly. 'But what about you? If
I am only a thing in his dream, what are *you*? You'll
go away, too!'

'Yes, *he* will go away, but *I* won't!' shouted
Tweedledee.

'Yes, *he* will go away, but *I* won't!' shouted
Tweedledum.

They shouted so loudly that Alice was afraid the
King might wake up. 'Don't make so much noise,' she
said to them.

'Why are *you* so afraid that he will wake up?' asked
Tweedledum. 'You are only one of the things in his
dream. You are not real.'

'I *am* real,' said Alice, and she began to cry.

'You won't make yourself real by crying,' said
Tweedledee. 'There is nothing to cry about.'

'I must be real,' said Alice. 'Only real people can cry!'

'Do you think those are real tears in your eyes?'
asked Tweedledee.

'I know they are just talking nonsense,' Alice
thought to herself, 'so I'm not going to cry about it.'
Then she said, 'I must be getting out of this forest.
Look! It's getting very dark. Do you think it is going
to rain?'

Tweedledum opened a large umbrella and put it up over himself and his brother. He looked up into it. 'No I don't think it is,' he said. 'Well, it's not going to rain under here.'

'But it might rain outside,' said Alice.   5

'It might if it wants to,' said Tweedledee. 'But we shall be nice and dry here, thank you!'

Alice was just going to say goodbye to them when Tweedledum jumped out from under the umbrella. He took hold of Alice's hand.   10

The broken rattle

'Do you see that?' he said. His face turned white, and his eyes turned yellow. He pointed with a shaking finger at a small thing lying under a tree. Alice looked and saw a baby's toy, a rattle.

'It's only a rattle,' said Alice, 'and it's broken.'

'I know it is,' said Tweedledum, and he began to run about angrily, pulling   25
his hair. 'It's broken. It's broken!' He looked at Tweedledee, who sat down on the ground and tried to cover himself with the umbrella.

Alice put her hand on his arm. She said, 'You don't   30
have to be so angry about an old rattle.'

'But it isn't old,' said Tweedledum, getting angrier and angrier. 'It's new, I tell you. I bought it yesterday. That's my nice new RATTLE.' And he began to scream and shout. 'A fight; we are going to have a fight.'

'Well, if you *want* to,' said Tweedledee, coming out from under the umbrella. 'But *she* must help us to dress up, you know.'

The brothers get ready to fight

5　The two brothers went off hand-in-hand into the forest. They returned in a minute with their arms full of things. There were buckets and plates and cloths and sticks and pieces of rope.

'Are you good at tying things together? All of these 10　have to go on us,' said Tweedledum.

Alice did her best. She tied the buckets and the cloths and all the other things around the two brothers. They looked very funny when she had finished.

'That will stop him from cutting my head off,' said 15　Tweedledee, as Alice tied a bucket over his head. 'It's not at all nice to have your head cut off, you know,' he said.

'Do I look very frightened?' asked Tweedledum, coming to have something tied over his head.

20　'Well, yes, a little,' replied Alice.

'Usually I'm very brave, but today I have a headache.'

'And I've got a toothache,' said Tweedledee.

'Well, you shouldn't fight today,' said Alice.

'No, we must have a fight, but we won't fight for very 25　long,' said Tweedledum. 'What's the time now?'

Tweedledee looked at his watch, and said 'Half past four.'

'Let's fight until six,' said Tweedledum.

'Yes, that's a good idea. And she can watch us. But 30　don't come too close,' Tweedledee shouted to Alice.

Alice began to laugh. 'And all this is because of a rattle!' she said.

'Well, it was a *new* rattle,' said Tweedledum. 'Quick,

we must start,' he said to his brother. 'It's getting dark.'

It was getting dark very quickly. Alice thought there must be a big storm coming. 'What a big black cloud that is,' she said. 'Look how fast it is coming! I think it has wings.'

'It's a big black bird,' shouted Tweedledum. And the two brothers ran away into the forest.

Alice talks to the White Queen

Alice ran a little way into the forest, too. Then she stopped under a large tree.

'That bird can never get me *here*,' she thought. 'It's too big to get in here under the trees. But I wish it wouldn't move its wings so quickly. It's making a strong wind under the trees. And what's that moving about in the wind? It looks like the thing that grandmother likes to wear over her shoulders when it's cold. Yes, it's a shawl.'

Alice caught the shawl as she spoke, and looked around for the owner. Just then the White Queen came running through the forest. Alice went to her with the shawl.

'I'm very glad I was here to catch it,' she said, as she put the shawl over the Queen's shoulders. The White Queen only looked at her in a funny way. She kept saying something to herself very quietly. It sounded like 'bread and butter, bread and butter'. 'Well,' thought Alice, 'perhaps I should be the first one to speak.' So she said, 'Am I talking to the White Queen?'

'Have you ever seen a Queen dressed like this?' the Queen replied, and tried to pull the shawl up over her. 'I've been trying to get dressed for the last two hours.'

The Queen looked very sad, so Alice asked, 'Can I help you?'

'I don't know what is wrong with this shawl,' the Queen said.

'I've tried to put it right many times, but it always goes wrong.'

'It *can* go straight,' said Alice, and she pulled the shawl straight. 'And look at your *hair*!' said Alice.

'The brush has got caught in it,' said the Queen, 'and I lost my comb yesterday.'

Alice took the brush out of the Queen's hair and tried to tidy it. 'Now you look better,' she said. 'You really should have a servant.'

'You can work for me,' replied the Queen. 'I'll give you two cents a week and jam to eat every second day.'

Alice began to laugh, and she said, 'I'm not looking for work, thank you, and I don't like jam.'

'It's very good jam,' said the Queen. 'It's made with lots of fresh fruit, and with plenty of sugar, you know.'

'Well, I don't want any today.'

'You *can't* have any jam today,' the Queen said. 'The rule is, jam every *second* day. That means jam tomorrow and jam yesterday, but never jam today.'

'But *sometimes* there must be jam *today*?' asked Alice.

'No. Never today. Every second day.'

'I don't understand,' said Alice.

'It's because we live backwards here,' said the Queen.

This Looking-Glass world gets stranger and stranger, thought Alice.

6

A SHEEP IN A SHOP

Alice feels like crying

It began to get lighter. 'That big black bird has flown away,' Alice said. 'I'm glad it has gone. I thought night was coming. But it really is very frightening here, isn't it. I feel like crying.'

'Don't cry,' said the Queen. 'Think what a clever girl you are. Think what a long way you have come today. Think what time it is. Think about anything, but please don't cry!'

Alice began to laugh when the Queen said this. She asked, 'Can you stop yourself crying by thinking things?'

'Yes, I can,' said the Queen, 'because nobody can do two things at the same time. Now let's begin with your age. How old are you?'

'I'm seven and a half,' said Alice.

'Well, I'm one hundred and one, five months and a day.'

'I can't believe *that*,' said Alice.

'Can't you?' asked the Queen. 'Well, try to believe it. Just shut your eyes and try.'

'It isn't possible. I can't believe it just by trying.'

'Yes, you can,' replied the Queen. 'When I was your age, I practised believing for half an hour a day. Sometimes, in one morning, I had believed six things that were not possible. Oh, there goes my shawl again.'

The wind had blown the Queen's shawl across another little stream. The Queen lifted up her arms and ran after it. Alice ran after the Queen.

'I've got it,' said the Queen. 'Now I will pin it on by myself. I was watching you, and I can do this much better now.'

The Queen becomes a sheep

'As the Queen spoke her voice began to change. 'Much be-etter. Much be-ee-etter. Be-e-e-h. Be-e-e-h!' Her voice sounded just like a sheep's voice. Alice looked at the Queen again. She saw that the Queen was covered in wool.

'Where am I?' Alice thought, and looked again. What had happened? Was she in a shop? And was that really a sheep, sitting on a chair in the corner?

Alice really was in a shop, and there in the corner was an old sheep. She was looking at Alice through her glasses, and holding lots of long, thin needles in her hands. They must be knitting needles, thought Alice. Yes, the old sheep was knitting.

'What do you want to buy?' asked the sheep, looking up from her knitting.

'I don't know yet,' replied Alice. 'Can I look around first?'

'You can look in front of you, and on both sides,' said the sheep, 'but you can't look all around you. You have not got eyes at the back of your head, have you?'

Alice looked around. The shop was full of lots of strange things. There were shelves on the walls with many different things on them. But something funny was happening. When Alice looked at something on a shelf to see what it was, suddenly *that* shelf became empty. All the *other* shelves were always full.

'Things seem to move around in this shop,' said Alice. She saw something that she thought was a doll. Every time she looked at it, it seemed to move to a different shelf. 'I know what I'll do,' Alice thought. 'I'll follow it up to the very top shelf. I am sure it will not go through the ceiling.' But it did!

On the river

'Are you a child or a toy?' asked the sheep. 'Why do you keep running round and round like that?' The sheep was now knitting with fourteen needles at the same time.

'I don't know how she can knit with all those needles,' Alice thought to herself.

'Can you row?' the sheep asked. She gave Alice a pair of knitting needles.

'Yes, a little — but not on land — and not with needles.' Alice was saying this, when suddenly the needles turned into oars. She and the sheep were in a little boat, going down a river. Alice had the oars in her hands.

'Feather,' said the sheep. She took up another pair of needles.

Alice didn't say anything. She did not know what to reply. She pulled on the oars. There was something strange about the water. Sometimes the oars got stuck and Alice couldn't lift them out.

'Feather! Feather!' the sheep called again, taking more needles. 'You'll catch a crab soon.'

'A nice little crab,' said Alice. 'that will be good.'

'Didn't you hear me say "feather"?' said the sheep angrily, taking some more needles.

'Yes, I did,' said Alice. 'You have said it many times. Now, where are the crabs?'

'In the water,' said the sheep. 'Feather!'

'Why do you always say "feather"?' asked Alice. 'I'm not a bird!'

'Yes, you are,' said the sheep. 'You are a silly goose.'

They didn't say anything for a minute or two. The boat moved on down the river.

Not long after this the oar got caught in something again and it *wouldn't* come out. Alice pushed and pulled. Suddenly it moved, and Alice fell off her seat into the bottom of the boat. The sheep said nothing at all and went on with her knitting. Luckily Alice wasn't hurt and she climbed back on to her seat.

Back in the shop

'You should have feathered,' said the sheep. 'I kept telling you to feather. That was a nice crab you caught.'

'Well, I didn't see it,' said Alice, looking down into the water. 'Are there many crabs here?'

'Yes, crabs and all sorts of things,' said the sheep. 'Now, what do you want to buy?'

'To *buy*?' asked Alice in surprise. She looked around and saw that she was in the little shop again. The boat and the oars and the river had all gone.

'Oh, can I buy an egg, please?' asked Alice. 'How much are they?'

'Five cents for one and two cents for two,' the sheep replied.

'Then two are cheaper than one,' said Alice.

'Yes, but you must eat them *both*, if you buy two,' said the sheep.

'Then I'll have one, please,' said Alice, and took out her money. The sheep put the money away in a box. 'You can get the egg yourself,' she said, and went to the other end of the shop.

'Oh,' said Alice. She moved around among the tables and chairs, looking for her egg. The shop was very dark, and the egg always seemed to be *very* far away. Alice couldn't get close to it.

'What's this thing? Is it a chair?' she asked. 'But it has branches and leaves on it. How strange to find trees growing in a shop. And here is a little stream. She stepped across it. 'Well, this is the strangest shop I have ever seen,' she thought.

So she went on, getting more and more surprised. Everything turned into a tree when she came close to it. She felt sure the egg would do the same.

HUMPTY DUMPTY

An egg like a man

As Alice got closer to the egg, it became bigger and bigger. It began to look less and less like an egg, and more and more like a man. When she was right up close
5 to it, Alice saw that it had eyes and a nose and mouth. Yes, it was HUMPTY DUMPTY himself! 'It can't be anybody else,' she said to herself. 'I'm sure it is him.'

Humpty Dumpty was sitting with his legs crossed on the top of a high wall. Alice was sure he was going
10 to fall off because the wall was not very thick.

Humpty Dumpty just looked in front of him. He didn't look at Alice at all. She thought he wasn't
15 really alive.

'He looks just like an egg,' she said. She was standing below him with her hands out to catch him, if he fell down.

'That's not a very nice thing to say,' said Humpty
20 Dumpty.

'I said you looked like an egg,' Alice explained politely. 'And some eggs are very pretty, you know.'

'Some people,' said Humpty Dumpty angrily, 'are as silly as a baby.'

Alice didn't know what to say to this. He wasn't talking   5
to her, she thought. When he spoke he was looking at a tree. Perhaps he was talking to the tree. So she stood and said a poem quietly to herself. Her mother had taught it to her:

> *Humpty Dumpty sat on a wall,*   10
> *Humpty Dumpty had a big fall,*
> *All the King's horses and all the King's men,*
> *Couldn't put Humpty Dumpty in his place again.*

'The last line is too long for the poem,' she said. She had forgotten that Humpty Dumpty would hear her.   15

The wall is very narrow

'Don't stand there talking to yourself like that,' Humpty Dumpty said, looking at her for the first time. 'Tell me your name and say what you want.'

'My name is Alice, but …'   20

'That's a silly name,' replied Humpty Dumpty. 'What does it mean?'

'Must a name mean something?' asked Alice.

'Yes, it must,' Humpty Dumpty said with a short laugh. '*My* name means the shape I am, and it is a very good   25
shape too. With a name like yours, you can be any shape at all.'

'Why do you sit out here all alone?' asked Alice.

'Because there is nobody here with me,' replied Humpty Dumpty. 'Did you think I didn't know the   30
answer to that? Ask another question.'

'Why don't you come down on to the ground? It's not very safe up there. The wall is very narrow.'

'Oh, I'm quite safe up here,' said Humpty Dumpty. 'I won't fall off. But if I *did* fall off, (and I never *will* fall off, you know), but if I *did* fall off, the King has promised me — to — to ...'

'To send all his horses and all his men,' said Alice.

'How did you know that?' shouted Humpty Dumpty angrily. 'You have been listening to what other people say, haven't you!'

'No, I haven't,' said Alice. 'I read it in a book.'

'Yes, well, perhaps they do write such things in a book,' said Humpty Dumpty. 'Now take a good look at me. I am someone who has spoken to a King. You may take my hand if you like.'

With a big smile that went from one ear to the other, he took Alice's hand. And he nearly fell off the wall.

An un-birthday present

Alice thought to herself, 'If he smiles any more, the two ends of his mouth might meet behind his head. Then I don't know what will happen. His *head* might fall off!'

'Yes, all the King's horses and all his men will come and put me together again,' said Humpty Dumpty. 'But now, what were we talking about?'

'I'm sorry but I can't remember,' said Alice politely.

'Well, we can start again then,' said Humpty Dumpty.

'All right,' said Alice. 'Let's talk about that nice belt you are wearing. Or is it a tie? No, a belt. I mean. I'm sorry but, is it a belt or a tie? Does it go round your stomach or your neck?'

Humpty Dumpty must have been angry to hear this. He said nothing for two minutes, then he replied. 'You must be very silly if you don't know the difference between a belt and a neck-tie. It's a neck-tie, child, and it's a beautiful one. It was given to me by the White King and Queen!'

'Really!' was all that Alice could say.

'Yes,' said Humpty Dumpty, putting his hands round his knees as he spoke. 'They gave it to me – for an un-birthday present.'

'Did you say an un-birthday present?' asked Alice.

'Yes, I did.'

'Well, I know what a *birthday* present is, but what is an un-birthday present?'

'It's a present you get when it *isn't* your birthday. That's all.'

'Oh,' said Alice. 'I think I like birthday presents best.'

'You don't know what you are talking about!' shouted Humpty Dumpty. 'How many days are there in a year?'

'Three hundred and sixty-five,' said Alice.

'And if you take one away from three hundred and sixty-five, what is left?'

'Three hundred and sixty-four, of course' said Alice.

'Would you write that down for me on a piece of paper,' said Humpty Dumpty. Alice smiled and wrote $365 - 1 = 364$.

Humpty Dumpty looked at what Alice had written and said, 'Yes, that seems to be right. Now if it is true, then there must be three hundred and sixty-four days every year when you can get un-birthday presents.'

'Yes,' said Alice.

'And only *one* for birthday presents.'

'I see,' said Alice.

'Do you like poems?' asked Humpty Dumpty. 'I know lots of very good poems.'

Alice was still thinking about un-birthday presents. She didn't really want to hear any more poems.

HUMPTY DUMPTY'S POEM

The little fishes of the sea

'The poem I have chosen for you is very funny,' said Humpty Dumpty. Alice thought it would be best for her to listen, so she said 'Thank you' and sat down.

5
> *'In Winter when the fields are white,*
> *I sing this song for your delight.*

'But I'm not singing it,' said Humpty Dumpty.
'No, you are not,' said Alice.

> *'In Spring when trees are turning green,*
10
> *I'll try and tell you what I mean.*

> *In Summer when the days are long,*
> *Perhaps you'll understand the song.*
> *In Autumn when the leaves are brown,*
> *Take pen and ink and write it down.'*

15
'I will if I can remember it,' said Alice. 'But Autumn is a very long time away.'
'You don't have to keep talking,' said Humpty Dumpty. 'You are stopping me from saying the poem.'
'I'm sorry,' said Alice.

20
> *'I sent a message to the fish,*
> *I told them "this is what I wish."*
> *The little fishes of the sea,*
> *They sent an answer back to me.*

The little fishes' answer was
"We cannot do it, Sir, because ..." '

'I don't understand,' said Alice.
'The rest of it is very easy,' Humpty Dumpty replied.

'I went to them again to say,   5
It will be better to obey.

The fishes answered with a grin,
"Why, what a temper you are in!"
I told them once, I told them twice,
They would not listen to advice.

I took a bucket, large and new,
Just right for what I had to do.
My heart went hop, my heart went thump
I filled the bucket at the pump

Then someone came to me and said,
"The little fishes are in bed."
I said to him, I made it plain,
"Then you must wake them up again."

I said it very loud and clear;
I went and shouted in his ear.'   20

Humpty Dumpty shouted loudly as he said the last
line.
Alice thought, 'I'm glad I wasn't the messenger!'

'But he was very stiff and proud,
He said, "You needn't shout so loud."   25

And he was very proud and stiff
He said "I'll go and wake them if ..."
I took my bucket from the shelf,
I went to wake them up myself.

5   *And when I found the door was locked,*
I pulled and pushed and kicked and knocked.
And when I found the door was shut
I tried to turn the handle but ...'

Alice says 'Goodbye'

10   Then there was a long silence.
'Is that all?' asked Alice politely.
'That is all,' said Humpty Dumpty. 'Goodbye.'
'This is very surprising,' Alice said to herself, but she thought it was time to go. So she got up and put out
15   her hand and said, 'Goodbye, I hope we meet again.'
'I don't think I will know who you are, if we do meet again,' said Humpty Dumpty. 'You just look like everyone else to me!'
'Well, just look at the face,' said Alice. 'Our faces are
20   usually different, you see.'
'But your face is the same as everyone else's,' said Humpty Dumpty. 'Two eyes, a nose in the middle and a mouth under it. It's always the same. Now if you had two eyes on the same side of your nose, or a
25   mouth at the top, it would be much easier for me to remember you.'
'I wouldn't look nice,' said Alice.
Humpty Dumpty just closed his eyes and said, 'Try it and see.'
30   Alice waited for a few minutes to see if he was going to speak again. But he did not open his eyes or say anything more. She said 'Goodbye' again, but he didn't

answer, so she walked quietly away. 'What a strange person,' she thought. 'I didn't understand him. And what did that silly poem mean?'

Suddenly, there was a very loud noise, and all the trees in the forest began to shake.   *5*

The King's horses and the King's men

Lots of soldiers came running through the forest. At first they came in twos and threes, then ten or twenty together, until they filled the whole forest.

Alice ran and stood behind a tree. She didn't want   *10* any of them to run over her. But the soldiers didn't seem to know what they were doing. They kept falling over each other. The ground was soon covered with soldiers, all lying on top of one another.

Then came the horses. They were a *little* better than   *15* the soldiers, because they had four feet. But they fell over each other too. As soon as a horse fell over, the man sitting on top of it fell off. Alice thought it was very, very funny. She was glad to get out of the forest and into an open place. There she saw the White King,   *20* writing in a book.

'I've sent them all,' he said, when he saw Alice. He looked very pleased with himself. 'Did you see any of my soldiers, as you came through the forest?'

'Yes, I did,' said Alice. 'Thousands of them, I think.'   *25*

'Four thousand, two hundred and seven,' said the King, looking in his book. 'I couldn't send all the horses, you know, because I need two of them for the game. And I haven't sent the two messengers either. They went to town. Look down the road. Can you see them?'   *30*

'No, I can't see anybody on the road,' said Alice. 'Oh, but *now* I can see somebody,' she said. 'It's a man. He's coming very slowly, but he does look funny.'

The King's messenger was running along the road, jumping into the air from time to time, and waving his hands like the wings of a bird.

'Yes, he runs like that when he is happy,' said the King. 'His name is Haffa. The other messenger is called Hatta. I must have two, you know, one to come and one to go. One to get things for me and one to take things for me.'

Haffa's news

Just then the messenger arrived. He had run so far that he couldn't say a word. He just stood in front of the King waving his hands about.

'Don't stand there like that. You are frightening me,' said the King, 'and I don't feel well. Give me a sandwich.'

The messenger opened a bag he was carrying and gave the King a sandwich. The King ate it very quickly.

'Do you have another one?' asked the King.

'There's nothing in my bag but pieces of paper.'

'Give me some paper then,' said the King. 'There's nothing like paper when you don't feel well. Did you pass anybody on the road?'

'I didn't *see* anybody.'

'Well, if you didn't *see* anybody, you couldn't *pass* anybody,' said the King. 'Now, tell us what is happening in the town.'

'I'll whisper it,' said the messenger, coming close to the King's ear. Alice thought, 'I won't be able to hear what he tells the King if he whispers.' But instead of whispering, the messenger shouted as loudly as he could, 'They are doing it again!'

'Do you call that a whisper?' said the King angrily.

'Who are doing it again?' asked Alice.

'The Lion and the Unicorn,' said the King.

THE LION AND THE UNICORN

The fight

Alice knew what a lion was. She was just going to ask
the King about a unicorn. Then she remembered she
had seen a picture of one in a story book. It was an
animal like a horse, but it had a big horn growing out   5
of its head.

'Are they fighting for the crown?' asked Alice.

'Yes, and it is *my* crown they are fighting for,' the
King replied. 'That's funny, isn't it? Let's go and watch
them.' So they hurried away. Alice sang a little song   10
she knew about the Lion and the Unicorn.

> *'The Lion and the Unicorn were fighting for*
> *the crown,*
> *The Lion chased the Unicorn all around the*
> *town,*   15
> *Some gave them white bread and some gave*
> *them brown,*
> *Some gave them fruit cake and chased them*
> *out of town.'*

After a time they came to a place where there were many people. The people were all watching the Lion and the Unicorn fighting. Alice and the King stood close to Hatta and the other messenger. Hatta was watching
5 the fight. He had a cup of tea in one hand and a piece of bread in the other.

'How are they getting on with the fight?' asked the King.

Hatta swallowed a large piece of bread, then he said,
10 'They are getting on very well. Each of them has been knocked down about eighty-seven times.'

'Well, they will soon bring the white bread and the brown bread, won't they?' asked Alice.

'It's ready for them now,' said Hatta. 'This is a piece
15 of it. It tastes good.'

The fighting stops

The Lion and the Unicorn were getting tired. They both sat down on the ground for a few minutes. The King called out, 'Ten minutes for a rest.'
20 Haffa and Hatta carried around pieces of brown and white bread for everyone to eat. Alice took a piece to try it, but it was *very* dry.

'I don't think they'll fight any more today,' said the King. Alice was watching the forest, and thought she
25 saw somebody coming. It was the White Queen. She came running out of the forest as fast as she could.

'Someone is chasing her,' said the King.

'Aren't you going to help her?' asked Alice.

'Oh, no. She can run faster than anybody,' said the
30 King.

Just then, the Unicorn walked past, with his hands in his pockets.

'I was the best today, I think,' he said to the King.

Then the Unicorn turned around quickly and saw
Alice. He looked at her for a minute. Then he asked,
   'What *is* that?'
   'It's a child,' Haffa replied. 'We found it today. Isn't
it pretty?'   5
   'I didn't think children were real,' said the Unicorn.
'I thought you only read about them in stories. Is
it alive?'
   'It can talk,' replied Haffa.

The Lion and the Unicorn meet Alice   10

The Unicorn looked carefully at Alice and then said,
'Talk, child.'
   Alice couldn't stop herself smiling. Then she said, 'Do
you know, I thought all unicorns were just in stories
too. I have never seen one alive before today!'   15
   'Well, now we have seen each other,' said the Unicorn.
'If you will believe in me, I will believe in you. Is that
all right?'
   'Yes, if you like,' said Alice.
   'And where is the fruit cake?' said the Unicorn to the   20
King. 'I don't want any brown bread.'
   'Yes, yes,' said the King. Then he whispered to Haffa,
'Open the bag.'
   Haffa took a large cake out of the bag. He gave it
to Alice. Then he took a dish and a knife out of the   25
bag.
   The Lion came to join them. He looked very tired
and sleepy, and his eyes were half shut. 'What is this?'
he asked, when he saw Alice. His voice sounded like
a bell, Alice thought.   30
   'It is a child,' said the Unicorn.
   'A child?' asked the Lion. 'Is that an animal or a
vegetable?'

'A child is a child,' said Alice.

'Then pass round the cake, child,' said the Lion, 'and sit down, both of you,' he said to the King and the Unicorn.

The King was feeling quite frightened sitting between the Lion and the Unicorn. He began to shake all over. The crown on his head began to shake too.

'We could have a lovely fight for the crown *now*,' said the Unicorn, looking at the crown on the King's head.

'I would win easily,' said the Lion.

'I don't think so,' said the Unicorn.

'But I chased you all around the town,' replied the Lion angrily.

The King was feeling more and more frightened, so he jumped up and asked, 'All around the town? That's a long way, isn't it? Did you go over the old bridge or did you go past the market place? I like the old bridge myself.'

'I don't remember,' said the Lion. 'Why is that child taking so long to cut the cake?'

Looking-Glass cake

Alice sat down near a little stream. She had the big dish on her knees. She began to cut the cake with the knife. 'It's very difficult,' she said to the Lion. 'Each time I cut off a piece, it joins itself back on to the cake again. Look.'

'You don't know how to cut Looking-Glass cake,' said the Unicorn. 'Take it round to everyone first, and then cut it up.'

This seemed to be nonsense to Alice, but she got up, carried the dish around, and the cake divided itself into three pieces. '*Now* cut it up,' the Lion said, as she returned to her place with the empty dish.

'This is not right,' the Unicorn suddenly shouted angrily. 'The child has given the Lion twice as much as me!'   5

'And she hasn't got any for herself,' said the Lion. 'Do you like fruit cake, child?' he asked.

But before Alice could reply, she heard a strange noise. It came from the town. It got louder and louder and seemed to go right through her head. It frightened   10 her so much that she began to run away. She came to the little stream, and jumped across it to the other side.

When she looked back she saw the Lion and the Unicorn standing up and looking around angrily to see what was happening. Alice put her hands over   15 her ears to keep out the noise.

'Well, *that* noise will chase them out of town, won't it?' she said to herself.

The White Knight

'Stop! Stop!'

After a time the noise seemed to go away. Everything was silent, so Alice lifted up her head to look around. There was no one.

5 'Was I dreaming about the Lion and the Unicorn, and those strange messengers?' she asked herself. But no; the big cake-dish was still there in front of her. 'So I can't be dreaming,' she said.

She thought about it some more. 'Perhaps we are all 10 part of the same dream. Oh, I *do* hope it's MY dream and not the Red King's. I don't like being in someone else's dream.'

Just then she heard a noise. Someone was shouting, 'Stop! Stop!' A Knight, dressed in red, came riding on 15 a horse, straight towards her. He was holding a club, a large thick metal stick, in his hand. 'You are my prisoner,' he said. He stopped his horse so quickly that he fell off.

Alice was more frightened for the Knight than for 20 herself. She watched him climb up on to his horse again.

'You are my …' he began, but then Alice heard another voice calling, 'Stop! Stop!' This time it was a White Knight. He, too, stopped his horse close to Alice, and 25 fell off. Then he got on it again.

The knights fight

The two knights sat looking at each other for some time without speaking. Alice looked at them. She didn't really know what to say.

'She is *my* prisoner, you know,' said the Red Knight.

'No, *I* saw her first. She is mine,' the White Knight replied.

'Well, we must fight for her, then,' said the Red Knight. He lifted up a strange-looking helmet that he was carrying, and put it on his head. It was in the shape of a horse's head. The White Knight did the same. Then they began to fight. Alice ran behind a tree to watch.

'They don't really know how to fight,' Alice thought as she watched them. One of the knights would lift up his club and try to hit the other with it. Then he would fall off his horse and have to climb up on to it again. The horses just stood there without moving. When the knights fell, they always seemed to fall on their heads.

After some time they stopped. The White Knight came up to Alice and said,

'That was a very good fight, wasn't it!'

'I don't know,' said Alice, 'I don't want to be anybody's prisoner. I want to be a Queen.'

'Well, you must cross the next stream to be a Queen,' said the White Knight. 'I'll come with you to the end of the forest, and then I must go back. That's all I'm allowed to do in this game, you know.'

'Thank you very much,' said Alice. 'Can I help you take that thing off your head?'

'You mean my helmet?' said the Knight. 'Yes, thank you.'

A box, a beehive and a mousetrap

Alice helped pull off the helmet from the White Knight's head. She saw that he was a little old man with long white hair. He had a kind face, and big eyes. He was wearing the strangest clothes Alice had ever seen.

The White Knight's clothes were all made of pieces of metal, and there was a funny little box tied across his shoulders. The box was not the right way up. It was open, and the lid was hanging down. Alice looked at it. She was going to ask what it was, when the Knight said, 'You like my little box, do you? I made it myself, to keep my clothes and sandwiches in. I put it this way up so the rain can't get in it.'

'But the things inside it will fall out!' said Alice. 'Do you know the lid is open?'

'Oh, I didn't know that,' said the Knight. 'So everything has fallen out of it! Well, I don't need the box now, do I?' So he took the box and threw it away into the trees.

'Do you know why I did that?' he asked Alice.

'No. Please tell me,' said Alice politely.

'So that the bees will come and live in it and make some honey.'

'Oh. That's what we call a beehive. But you have a beehive already.' 5

Alice pointed to a beehive, which was tied to the White Knight's horse.

'Yes, I know. It's a very good beehive. But no bees have come to live in it yet. And do you know what this is?' he asked. 10

'Isn't that something to catch mice with — a mousetrap?'

'Yes, it's a mousetrap,' replied the Knight. 'But I haven't caught a mouse yet.

Perhaps the bees chase the mice away, or the mice chase the bees away. One or the other.' 20

'You won't find any mice on a horse's back, will you?' asked Alice.

Ready for everything

'Perhaps not. But if they *do* come, I'll be ready for them,' said the Knight. 'You must be ready for *everything*, 25 you know. Look at these things round my horse's feet.

Do you know what they are for?' he asked. He was pointing to some pieces of metal that were tied to the horse's feet.

'No, what are they for?' asked Alice.

'To stop the fish biting my horse's feet,' replied the Knight. 'I made them myself, too. But tell me, what is that dish for?' he said to Alice.

'It's for the fruit-cake,' said Alice.

'We'll take it with us,' said the Knight. 'It will be useful if we find a fruit-cake. Help me put it in this bag.'

He held open a large bag, and tried to lift the dish into it. He nearly fell into it himself the first two times he tried. Then he tied the bag behind him, on the horse.

'I hope your hair is well tied on,' he said to Alice, as they walked through the forest.

'So do I,' Alice replied. 'Why?'

'Well, the wind is very strong here. It might blow your hair away.'

'And have you made anything to stop the wind blowing away people's hair?' asked Alice.

'Not yet,' replied the Knight. 'But I have made something to stop your hair *falling* off,' he said.

'Please tell me about it,' said Alice.

'Well, first you take a stick. Then you make all your hair grow up the stick, like a fruit tree. Now, the reason hair falls off is because it hangs *down*. Things never fall *up*, you know. Why don't you try it?'

A strange horse-rider

Alice thought about it as they walked, but she really didn't want to try it. She had to help the old Knight a lot, because he was not a very good rider.

Each time the horse stopped, he fell off in front of
it. When the horse started again, he fell off the back
of it. Sometimes he fell off the sides of the horse as
well. Alice thought it was best not to walk too close.
She didn't want the Knight to fall on her!   5

'You are not really a very good rider, are you?'
said Alice, after the Knight had fallen off for the
fifth time.

'Why do you say that?' asked the Knight, as he
climbed back on to the horse.   10

'Well, people don't fall off horses so often, if they
are good at riding them.'

'But I *am* good at riding. I have been riding horses
for many years,' said the Knight. He closed his eyes
as he spoke and the horse walked on quietly.   15

'Yes. If you want to be a good rider like me —,' he
said, waving his arms around him as he spoke. Then
before he could say anything more, he fell off the
horse again. He fell on his head, right in front of the
horse.   20

'Oh, I hope you haven't broken any bones,' said
Alice, helping him on to the horse again.

'Oh, not very many,' said the Knight. 'Now, as I was
saying, if you want to be a good rider, you must learn
to sit on the horse when it is moving.' He began to   25
wave his hands around again. This time he fell off
the horse on to his back.

Alice couldn't stop herself from laughing. 'You
make so many things,' she said. 'Why don't you
make something to stop yourself falling off a horse?'   30

'Perhaps I will,' said the Knight.

Alice ran to help him. When she stood him on his
feet again, he went on talking more nonsense than
ever. A little while later they came to the end of the
forest.   35

THE KNIGHT'S SONG

The little man

Alice wanted to thank the Knight for taking her to the end of the forest. But before she could speak he said to her, 'Do you want to hear a song?'

'Is it very long?' Alice asked. She thought that she had heard quite enough long poems for one day.

'It *is* long,' said the Knight, 'but it is very, very beautiful. When you hear it, it will either make you cry, or ...'

'Or what?' asked Alice.

'Or it *won't*,' said the Knight. 'It's called "Sitting on a Gate".'

'I don't think I know it,' said Alice.

'I wrote the music myself, too,' said the Knight. And then he began to sing:

> *'I'll tell you everything I can,*
> *I hope you won't be late,*
> *About a little man I found,*
> *Sitting on a gate.*
> *"Tell me who you are," I asked,*
> *"And tell me how you live."*
> *This is what he said to me,*
> *This answer he did give.*
>
> *He said "I look for butterflies,*
> *That fly around my feet.*
> *I make them into butter cakes,*
> *And sell them in the street,*
> *I sell them to the men who sail*
> *The rivers and the seas,*

That's how I make my money, so
Why don't you buy some, please?"

But I was thinking of a way
To make my hair turn green,
Then I would wear a large white hat   5
So it could not be seen.
And having no reply to give
To what the old man said,
I asked "Please tell me how you live,"
And hit him on the head.   10

He said, "I look for fishes' eyes,
That shine so blue and bright,
I make them into buttons,
And I work all through the night.
But these I do not sell for gold,   15
Or silver coins that shine,
One small brown cent is all I ask,
For that I'll give you nine."

But I was thinking of a way
To feed myself on cake,   20
And so go on from day to day
Without a pain or ache.
I shook him well from side to side,
Until his face was blue,
"Come, tell me how you live," I cried,   25
"And tell me what you do!"

"I sometimes dig for sandwiches,
And sometimes look for crabs,
I sometimes search the countryside
For wheels of cars and cabs,   30
And that is what I've always done,

(It's true, I'm very old),
That's why I haven't got a house,
That's why I have no gold."

So now if ever I am sad,
5 *Which happens every day,*
If someone tells me I am bad,
Or trouble comes my way,
Or if I drop a heavy box,
Upon my largest toe,
10 *I cry because I think about*
That man I used to know.

Whose eyes were kind,
Whose words were slow,
Whose hair was whiter than the snow,
15 *Whose body never seemed to grow,*
Whose head was always very low,
The man I met so long ago,
Sitting on a gate.'

The Knight says 'Goodbye'

20 As the Knight sang the last words of his song, he pulled the horse's head around and started off down the road. 'You don't have very far to go,' he said to Alice. 'Just walk down the hill and cross over the little stream. Then you will be a Queen. I must say
25 goodbye now.'

'Goodbye,' said Alice, 'and thank you for the song. I liked it very much.'

'But you didn't cry very much,' said the Knight.

The Knight rode away on his horse. Alice watched
30 him go. Every minute or so he fell off and had to climb back on his horse again. Then he waved, and turned

a corner, and Alice could see him no longer.

'Now I shall cross that little stream and become a Queen,' said Alice.

She ran down to the stream, and stepped across.

Alice is a Queen

When she was on the other side of the stream, she sat down on a nice piece of grass. Flowers were growing everywhere. She lay down on the grass for a minute to rest and to think.

Suddenly she found something heavy on her head. 'What is this?' she asked herself, and put her hands up to touch it. Then she took it off to look at it. It was a crown, and the crown was made of gold.

'How nice to be a Queen,' said Alice to herself. 'But a Queen shouldn't be sitting on the grass like this!'

She got up and walked about. She walked quite carefully, because she didn't want the crown to fall off. She didn't see anybody watching so she walked around and around, just like a Queen.

When she sat down again she found that the Red Queen and the White Queen were sitting on each side of her. She didn't understand where they had come from, but she didn't think it would be polite to ask.

She *did* want to know if the game was finished or not. She said, 'Please tell me …' The Red Queen looked at her angrily.

'Speak when someone speaks to you!' she said.

Alice thought for a minute and then she replied, 'But if *everyone* did that nobody would ever say anything. If *you* only spoke when you were spoken to and the other person always waited for *you* to begin, who would start doing the talking?'

'How silly!' said the Queen. 'You don't understand.'

Then after she had been thinking for a while, she began to talk about something else.

'Who said you were a Queen? You can't be a Queen until you have passed the examination. We must start soon!'

'Did you know there will be a party?' asked the White Queen. 'I invite you to come to Alice's party this afternoon.'

The Red Queen smiled and said, 'Thank you. And I invite you, too.'

Alice thought a party would be nice. It would be better than an examination. She said, 'I didn't know I was going to have a party. If I am, then I think I should do the inviting!'

QUESTIONS AND ANSWERS

A Looking-Glass world examination

'You think too much,' said the Red Queen. 'But let's see if you are clever at addition. What's one and one and one and one and one and one and one and one and one and one and one and one?' She spoke very quickly. 5

'I can't remember all that,' said Alice.

'Well, she can't do addition,' said the White Queen. Let's try some subtraction. Can you do subtraction? Take nine from eight.' 10

'Nine from eight! I can't, you know,' replied Alice, 'But . . .'

'She can't do subtraction,' said the White Queen. 'Can you do division? Divide a loaf of bread by a knife. What's the answer to that?' 15

'Well, it must be ...' Alice began, but the Red Queen answered for her. 'Bread and butter. Now answer this. Take a bone from a dog and what remains?'

Alice thought for a minute again. Then she said, 'Well, the bone wouldn't remain, if I took it. And the 20 dog wouldn't remain. It would come to bite me. And I'm sure I wouldn't remain.'

'Then you think nothing would remain?' said the Red Queen.

'I think that's the answer,' said Alice. 25

'You are wrong,' said the Red Queen. 'The dog would be angry, and his *anger* would remain.'

Alice thought to herself, 'We always seem to talk nonsense here.'

Now it was time for Alice to ask a question. 'Can *you* do addition?' she asked the White Queen suddenly.

The Queen shut her eyes. 'I can do addition, if you give me enough time, but I can't do subtraction.'

'Do you know your ABC?' asked the Red Queen.

'Yes, I do,' replied Alice.

'So do I,' said the White Queen, 'and if you are good, I'll teach you how to read words of *one* letter!'

'Can you speak French?' asked the Red Queen. 'What's the French for Fiddle-de-dee?'

'Fiddle-de-dee is not English,' replied Alice.

'I didn't say it was,' said the Queen.

'Well, you tell me what language Fiddle-de-dee is,' answered Alice. 'Then I'll tell you how to say it in French.'

The Red Queen stood up very straight and said, 'Queens never make bargains.'

'I wish Queens never asked questions,' Alice thought to herself.

The storm last Tuesdays

'And did you see the storm last Tuesdays?' asked the White Queen.

'You mean last Tuesday. Not last Tuesdays,' said Alice.

'Oh, no. Tuesdays. Here we sometimes have three days or three nights all together. And sometimes in the winter we have as many as five nights all at the same time. It's to keep us warm, you know.'

'Are five nights warmer than one night?' asked Alice.

'Yes, they are five times as warm.'

'But they should be five times as *cold!* ' said Alice.

'Yes. Five times as warm and five times as cold. Just as I am five times as rich as you are, and five times as clever.'

'More nonsense again,' thought Alice.

'Oh, it was such a bad storm,' the White Queen began again. 'Some of the ceiling fell down. Lots of thunder came in, and it went all over the room — big pieces of thunder you know — and all the tables and chairs fell over. I was so frightened I forgot my own name.'

The Queens go to sleep

Just then she put her head on Alice's shoulders and said, 'I am feeling very, very sleepy.'

'She is tired,' said the Red Queen. 'Why don't you sing her a song?'

'I don't know any nice songs,' said Alice.

'Well, I shall sing one myself,' said the Red Queen, and she began:

'Listen, my lady, I'll sing you a song,
You sleep with Alice, your day has been long.
We'll go to the party, we'll dance all night through,
Red Queen and White Queen and Queen Alice too.

'And now you know the words,' she said, and she put her head down on Alice's other shoulder. 'You sing it this time. I'm feeling tired too.' And soon both the Queens were asleep.

'What shall I do?' thought Alice. 'I've never had to look after *two* Queens before, and I'm sure nobody else has either. No, I'm sure I've never read about it in a book. Please wake up. Please wake up, Queens,' she said. But there was no answer.

Queen Alice's door

Alice sat listening to the Queens sleeping, when suddenly they were gone. She found herself standing in front of a door. QUEEN ALICE was written in big letters over the door. There were also two little bells. One had 'Visitor's Bell' written over it, and the other had 'Servant's Bell' over it.

5   'Which bell should I ring?' Alice asked herself. 'I'm not a visitor and I'm not a servant.' Just then the door opened a little. A head looked out. It was very long, quite like a bird. It said, 'Nobody can come in until the week after next week.' The door closed again.

10   Alice knocked on the door many times, but no-one came. She did not know what to do. Then a big old frog walked up. He was wearing yellow clothes and very big boots.

'What do you want?' he asked in a deep voice.

15   'Who is going to open this door? Where has the servant gone?' asked Alice angrily.

'Which door?' asked the frog.

'This door, of course!' shouted Alice. 'I've been knocking for so long.'

20   'Knocking?' said the frog. 'You shouldn't do that: makes it angry!' The frog looked at the door with his big eyes for a minute. Then he kicked it hard, and the door opened.

Alice heard a voice singing:

25   *"Oh, Looking-Glass world," it was Alice who said,*
"Today I'm a Queen, I've a crown on my head.
I'm having a party, I hope you will come,
All Looking-Glass people, please join in the fun."'

Then Alice heard lots of voices singing:

30   *'We'll go to the party, and what shall we take?*
Sandwiches, ice-cream, apples and cake,
Put cats in the coffee and mice in the tea,
And welcome Queen Alice, thirty-times-three.'

A party

Then Alice heard lots of voices shouting and singing loudly. Some people were shouting 'Welcome, Queen Alice.'

'I think I'll go inside,' thought Alice, and she walked in. Inside there was a very big table, and sitting round it were animals and birds and even some flowers.

'I'm glad they have all come, because I wouldn't really know who to invite,' thought Alice. There were three chairs at the top of the table. The Red and White Queens were already sitting in two of them, but the middle one was empty. Everyone was silent as Alice sat down. Then the Red Queen spoke.

'You missed the soup and the fish,' she said. 'Bring the meat.' Someone carried a large dish of meat and put it on the table in front of Alice.

'Have you met the meat?' asked the Red Queen. 'Alice — Meat. Meat — Alice.' The meat stood up on the plate and made a little bow to Alice. Alice returned the bow, thinking, 'This is the first time I have ever bowed to a piece of meat!'

'Can I cut you a piece of meat?' asked Alice, looking at the Red and the White Queens.

'No, thank you. It isn't polite to eat anyone you have met, is it?' said the Red Queen. 'Take the meat away! Bring the cake!'

So they took away the meat and brought a large plate with a cake on it. Alice was just going to cut it, when the cake said, 'How would you like me to cut a piece out of you, child?'

Alice didn't know what to say to this, so she sat silently looking at the cake.

The White Queen spoke. 'Let's all drink to Alice. Let's wish her good health. Take your glasses!'

Everyone began drinking, but how funny they looked! Some of them put their glasses on their heads and the wine ran down all over their faces. Some turned over their glasses on the table and drank from the top of the table.

'Now you should say something to thank them!' said the Red Queen.

'We will help you,' said the White Queen. Then the two Queens began pushing Alice, one on one side and one on the other.

'So this is how they want to help me,' thought Alice. 'They want to push the words out of my mouth.'

SHAKING AND WAKING

Something happens

Alice started speaking to the Looking-Glass people. 'I want to thank you all,' she began, but the Queens were pushing her so hard that she started to rise into the air. She had to hold on to the table to pull herself down again.

'Be careful!' shouted the White Queen, and suddenly took hold of Alice's hair. 'Something is going to happen.'

And then all sorts of things *did* start to happen. The bottles started to join themselves to the plates and fly around the room. Then a horse began to laugh. Alice looked at the White Queen, but she could only see a large piece of meat sitting in the White Queen's chair. Next, she heard the White Queen's voice coming from out of the soup dish. 'Here I am,' said the Queen, and Alice saw the Queen's face smiling at her from under the soup.

'I've had enough of all this,' said Alice loudly. And she stood up. She took the table-cloth in her hands and pulled it as hard as she could. And when she pulled it, the plates, the dishes, the knives and forks and all the people fell on to the floor.

Alice turned to the Red Queen.

'And now for *you!*' she began, because she was sure the Red Queen was the cause of all the trouble. But the Queen was gone. Alice saw her running around the top of the table. She was as small as a doll now. She was chasing after her shawl.

'You! You!' shouted Alice.
'I'm going to shake you until you turn into
a kitten! That's what I am going to do with you!'
   Alice lifted the Queen off the table as she spoke,
5 and began to shake her as hard as she could. The Red
Queen said nothing. But her face grew very small and
her eyes got large and green. And as Alice went on
shaking her, she got shorter — and fatter — and softer
— and rounder — and ...

10 — and it really was a kitten!

Who dreamed it?

'Oh, please don't make that noise, Red Queen,' said
Alice to the kitten. 'I was having a very nice dream,
and you woke me. But you went with me, didn't you,
15 Kitty, into the Looking-Glass world.' Alice looked
among the chess pieces on the table and picked up
the Red Queen. Then she sat down on the floor with
the kitten and put the Red Queen in front of her.

'There, Kitty, this was what you turned into, wasn't it!' Then she saw that Dinah, the mother cat, was still washing the white kitten. 'Haven't you finished with the White Queen yet?' she asked.

'You shouldn't do that to a *Queen*, Dinah,' Alice went on. 'But Dinah, who were you in my dream? Were you Humpty Dumpty? I think you were, but I'm not sure, so I won't tell your friends about it.

'Oh, Kitty, I know what you would like in the Looking-Glass world. I heard some poems about fish! Tomorrow I will give you some fish to eat. And I will tell you the poem – "The Walrus and the Carpenter". I hope the fish tastes as nice as the oysters.

'But Kitty, tell me *who* dreamed it all? Listen carefully when I talk to you, and don't go on washing yourself like that. You see, Kitty, it must have been *me*, or the Red King. He was part of my dream, wasn't he, but I was part of his dream too. Was it the Red King? You were his wife, I think, so I'm sure you know.'

But the kitten just went on washing herself. It pretended it had not heard Alice's question.

Who do *you* think did the dreaming?

QUESTIONS AND ACTIVITIES

CHAPTER 1

Choose the right words to say what the chapter is about: **floor, pawn, wind, wall, table, clock, daughter, fire.**

In the Looking-Glass room Alice saw a (1) _____ that was burning brightly. The pictures on the (2) _____ seemed to be alive. The (3) _____ had a smiling face. The chess pieces on the (4) _____ were moving about.

A (5) _____ was lying on the table, crying like a baby. Alice picked the Queen up, and put her down beside her little (6) _____. The Queen thought a strong (7) _____ had blown her up on to the (8) _____.

CHAPTER 2

Put the beginning of each sentence with the right ending.

1 The Tiger Lily said flowers talked   or she would pick them.
2 The Rose said they didn't like to   other flowers could not speak.
3 Alice told the flowers to be quiet,   speak first because it wasn't polite.
4 Alice asked why asleep.   they were always
5 The Tiger Lily said it was because   when there was somebody to talk to.

CHAPTER 3

Put the paragraphs in the right order.

1 When they left the wood the deer knew that it was a deer, and that Alice was a child. It became frightened and ran away quickly.
2 When Alice was in the wood she could not remember the name of anything.

3 The deer spoke to Alice. It asked Alice what she called herself, but Alice could not remember. The deer could not remember its own name, either.

4 A deer came and looked at Alice with big friendly eyes. Alice held out her hand and tried to touch it.

CHAPTER 4

The underlined sentences are all in the wrong paragraph. Which paragraph should they go in? Write them out in the right place.

1 The sun was shining in the middle of the night. <u>The Walrus and the Carpenter sat down on some flat rocks.</u> There were no clouds in the sky, or birds flying through the air.

2 The Walrus and the Carpenter were walking along the shore. <u>Then the Walrus and the Carpenter began to eat the little Oysters.</u> They asked some Oysters to go for a walk with them.

3 Many young Oysters left the sea and came to the shore. <u>They were crying because there was too much sand.</u> The little Oysters stood waiting in a row.

4 The Walrus said he needed some bread and some salt and pepper. <u>The moon said that the sun was very rude.</u> When it was time to go home, they had eaten all of them.

CHAPTER 5

Choose the right words to say what this chapter is about.

1 Tweedledum was **angry/hungry** because his toy was broken.

2 He wanted to **bite/fight** Tweedledee.

3 Tweedledee said he had a **headache/toothache**.

4 They said they would not fight for **long/wrong**, only until six o'clock.

CHAPTER 6

The letters in these words are all mixed up. What should they be? (The first one is 'voice').

The queen's (1) **ecivo** began to change. She was covered in (2) **lowo**. She changed into an old (3) **epesh**.

Alice thought she was in a (4) **hops**. She saw the old sheep, sitting in a (5) **nerroc**. The sheep was looking at Alice, and (6) **ginttink**.

CHAPTER 7

Put Humpty Dumpty's words in the right order.

1   Alice said that Humpty Dumpty looked just like an egg.
     He said [a very nice thing] [was not] [that] [say] [to].
2   Alice asked him why he sat out there all alone.
     He said [because] [with him] [that] [there was nobody] [was].
3   Alice asked him why he didn't come down on to the ground.
     He said [up on the wall] [that he] [quite safe] [was] [sitting].
4   Alice asked him if the thing he was wearing was a tie or a belt.
     He said [it] [neck-tie] [was] [that] [a].

CHAPTER 8

Put the sentences in the right order to say what the chapter is about. The first one has been done for you.

1   Suddenly there was a very loud noise.
2   They kept falling over and lying on top of one another.
3   Soon the ground was covered with soldiers.
4   The trees in the forest began to shake.
5   The soldiers didn't seem to know what they were doing.
6   More and more soldiers started coming into the forest.

CHAPTER 9

Who did these things? Choose from: **the White Queen, Hatta, the Unicorn,** *or* **Alice.**

1   _____ sang a little song.
2   _____ had a cup of tea in one hand and bread in the other.
3   _____ came running out of the forest as fast as she could.
4   _____ didn't think that children were real.

CHAPTER 10

There is something wrong in the underlined part of all these sentences: use the following words to correct them: **little, feet, eyes, white, metal.**

1 The White Knight <u>was a tall old man</u>.
2 He <u>had long brown hair</u>.
3 He <u>had a kind face and big ears</u>.
4 His clothes <u>were made of pieces of wool</u>.
5 There were some pieces of metal <u>tied to the horse's neck</u>.

CHAPTER 11

Some of these sentences are true, but others are false. Which are the false ones?

1 The Knight told Alice that she had far to go.
2 Alice would be a Queen when she crossed over the little stream.
3 The Knight rode away on his horse.
4 He kept falling off his horse and having to climb back on.
5 Alice stepped across the stream and then sat down on a chair.
6 Suddenly she found something heavy on her shoulders.
7 When she took it off to look at it, she saw it was a golden crown.

CHAPTER 12

Join the beginnings of these sentences to the correct endings.

1 Alice heard a lot of voices	sitting round a big table.
2 Inside she saw animals, birds and flowers	wished her good health.
3 The Red Queen and the White Queen	shouting and singing loudly.
4 Everyone drank to Alice and	were sitting in two chairs.

CHAPTER 13

Choose the right words to say what the chapter is about.

1 Many **funny/strange/frightening** things began to happen.
2 The bottles and plates started to **run/walk/fly** around the room.
3 A horse began to **laugh/talk/sing**.
4 The Red Queen changed into a **unicorn/kitten/flower.**

Oxford
Progressive
English Readers